DISNEP PRESENTS A PIXAR FILM

Cars

The Junior Novelization

D0980755

Disne**y** PRESENTS A **PIXAR** FILM

The Junior Novelization

Adapted by Lisa Papademetriou

Random House New York

Excitement pulsed through a packed stadium where thousands of revved-up fans gathered to watch the Dinoco 400—the biggest race of the year. They honked their horns and waved their flags in support of their favorite racers. The winner would receive the Piston Cup trophy and be crowned champion for the entire season!

While more fans cheered outside, Lightning McQueen, the rookie, was parked in the back of his posh trailer, trying to psych himself up for the race. It had been a huge year for McQueen. He had exploded onto the racing scene like a stick of dynamite, and he already had an impressive list of wins and top finishes. He knew that he had a good shot at winning the Dinoco 400, and if he did, he would be the first rookie in history to do it. McQueen felt his rpm increase at the thought.

"Focus." He concentrated hard. "Speed. I am speed. I eat losers for breakfast. I am Lightning." He had two things on his mind: winning and all the perks that came with it, including the Dinoco sponsorship. The sponsorship meant that Dinoco would pay McQueen a lot of money to compete in races.

"Hey, Lightning," called Mack. He was McQueen's loyal trailer driver. "You ready?"

McQueen could feel the roar of the crowds in the stands as his tires buzzed.

"Oh, yeah!" The sleek red race car revved his engine. "Lightning's ready."

Cameras flashed across the stands like fireworks as McQueen rolled off the rear of his trailer. He made sure he gave them a good look at his lucky lightning bolt sticker and the number 95 on his side.

"Ka-chow!" he called out as his grill flashed across the stadium's giant video screen.

McQueen made his way to the track. His competitors were waiting. There were more than forty other cars in the race, but Lightning McQueen knew that he had to worry about only two of them. Strip Weathers—also known as The King—had won more Piston Cups than any other car in history. He also had been Dinoco's golden boy for years, getting all those big paychecks. This would be his last race before retiring. McQueen was sure that The King wanted to go out on top, and he still had the speed to do it.

And then there was Chick Hicks. He was famous for battling through the line—bashing any car who stood in his way. He had never managed to beat The King, though. He was more determined than ever to win and begin a new era—the Chick era.

"Bob, my oil pressure's through the roof right now!" cried Darrell Cartrip, one of the race announcers. Poor Darrell was in danger of overheating as the green flag dropped. The three rivals lurched into high gear, launching the greatest race of the decade as they roared across the starting line.

"Right you are, Darrell," Bob Cutlass agreed as

he watched the action from the announcers' booth. "The winner of this race will win the season title *and* the Piston Cup!"

"The legend, the runner-up, and the rookie," Darrell said. "Three cars, one champion."

Lightning McQueen poured on the speed as The King's sleek tail fin flashed around the track with Chick right behind it. McQueen punched the gas and flew ahead of Chick. But Chick Hicks wasn't about to lose this race to a rookie. Coming up fast, he slammed McQueen's rear and spun him onto the infield.

The crowd gasped as McQueen whirled out of control on the grass.

McQueen recovered quickly, tearing up the field as he zipped back onto the track. But now he was in last place! He pushed hard to make up the time.

Still, Chick wasn't going to let McQueen close in on him. He wasn't taking any chances. "Dinoco is all mine!" he cried as he slammed into the car beside him, sending it spinning out of control. In an instant, other cars began to crash into a pileup. "Get through *that*, McQueen!" With a confident sneer, the ruthless race car headed into the pits for fuel and service.

McQueen tried to go around the wreckage, but it was impossible. With no other choice, he did the only thing he could think of: he went through it! Dodging rubble and smoke, McQueen moved spectacularly, gliding between stopped vehicles and leapfrogging into the air over a pile of cars.

"McQueen made it through!" shouted Chick's crew chief.

And McQueen didn't stop. While everyone else headed into the pits, he kept rolling . . . right into first place!

"Woo-hoo!" McQueen cried.

"You know, the rookie just fired his crew chief," Darrell announced. "That's the third one this season!"

"Well, he says he likes working alone, Darrell!" Bob said.

Chick and The King bolted out of pit row and didn't waste any time in trying to catch up with McQueen. The laps flew by, and it looked as if no one would beat him. Finally, McQueen headed into the pits for fuel. He couldn't win the race on fumes.

"No, no, no—no tires!" he shouted as his crew tried to replace his worn tires. There wasn't any time. "Just the gas!"

"Looks like it's all gas 'n' goes for McQueen today!" Darrell observed as he peered down at pit row below him. "Now, normally I'd say that's a short-term gain, long-term loss, but it sure is working for him."

The frenzied crowd's excitement grew as the contenders sped around the track. Then the white flag waved.

LAST LAP, read the stadium's giant video monitor.

"Checkered flag," McQueen said to himself, "here I come."

Ka-blam!

"Oh, no," Darrell cried as he watched the rookie lose speed. "McQueen has blown a tire!"

Chick and The King pounded ahead, making up time with every second. But McQueen didn't give up. He plunged forward. . . .

Ka-blam!

He lost another tire!

"Come on!" Determined to win, McQueen

struggled forward, limping on his rear wheel rims.

"I don't believe what I'm watching!" Darrell cried. "Lightning McQueen is a hundred feet from his Piston Cup—"

"The King and Chick are coming on strong!" Bob shouted. "McQueen's nearly there, but Chick and The King are almost caught up!"

McQueen dragged himself forward. He was inches away from crossing the finish line—and making history. He could hear Chick and The King coming up behind him. In a last-ditch effort, McQueen took a giant leap and slid forward. He even stuck out his tongue to gain an extra inch.

"It's too close to call!" Bob announced as he gaped at the photo finish. "The most spectacular, amazing, incomprehensible, unequivocably unbelievable ending in the history of the world, and we don't even know who won!"

McQueen let his pit crew fit him with a new set of tires while the referees reviewed the instant replay. The rookie wasn't worried; he was positive he had the race in the bag.

"We're here in Victory Lane awaiting the race results," announced a reporter as she thrust a microphone into McQueen's grill. "McQueen, that was quite a risky move, not taking tires. Are you sorry you don't have a crew chief?"

McQueen gave her a cocky smile. "No, I'm not," he replied. "'Cause I'm a one-man show."

The reporter turned to the camera. "That was a very confident Lightning McQueen, coming to you live from Victory Lane."

"Yo, Chuck," McQueen called to one of his pit crew, who struggled to replace the blown tires.

"Chuck! What are you doing? You're blocking the camera. Everyone wants to see the bolt," he said, referring to his lucky lightning bolt sticker. Suddenly, the jack flew out from underneath McQueen. *Ka-thunk!* He hit the ground hard.

"Whoa," he called as the pittie rolled off, "where are you going?"

"I quit, Mr. One-Man Show!" the pittie spat.

"Oh, oh, okay, leave!" McQueen grinned at the camera. "Fine!" He snorted and added sarcastically, "How will I ever find anyone else who knows how to fill me up with gas? Adios, Chuck!"

"And my name's not Chuck!" the pittie hollered.

"Whatever," McQueen scoffed. Plenty of pit crews had quit on him before, but Lightning McQueen didn't care. He knew that when it came to racing, he was the only one who mattered.

"Hey, Lightning," Chick called as he rolled up to his rival. "Yo, McQueen. Seriously, that was some pretty darn nice racing out there . . . by *me*."

"Good one!" his pit crew said, cracking up at the lame joke. "Oh, yeah! Zinger!"

"Welcome to the Chick era, baby," Chick went

on, his voice glossy with confidence. "The Piston Cup, it's mine, dude, it's mine. Hey, fellas, how do you think I'd look in Dinoco blue?"

"Blue's your color," one of the pitties piped up.

"In your dreams," McQueen replied, "thunder."

"Yeah, right, *thunder*," Chick said, turning to his pit crew. "What's he talking about, 'thunder'?"

"Hey, you know," McQueen shot back, "because thunder always comes after lightning! *Ka-pow!*" McQueen flashed his shiny lightning bolt sticker at the crowd again, and the reporters went wild. They squeezed in around him, angling for a photo of the famous race car. "McQueen, over here!" "This way, McQueen!" "Hey, McQueen, we want to see the bolt!"

"Ka-ching!" McQueen said with each new pose for the cameras. *"Ch-ch-chkow!"*

Chick turned to his pit crew as the reporters elbowed him and his crew out of the way. "Who here knew about the *thunder* thing?" he demanded.

The King stood nearby, surrounded by his loyal Dinoco pit crew.

"You sure made Dinoco proud, King," said

Dinoco's owner, Tex, to the longtime champion.

"My pleasure, Tex," The King replied.

The King's wife snuggled against his fender. "Whatever happens," she said gently, "you're a winner to me, you ol' daddy rabbit."

"Thanks, dear," the veteran said lovingly. "Wouldn't be nothin' without you." Then he rolled over to McQueen, who was surrounded by adoring fans. The King knew that McQueen was arrogant, but he respected McQueen's talent. He wanted to help the kid.

"Hey, buddy," The King said once the reporters had cleared away, "you're one gutsy racer. You got more talent in one lug nut than a lotta cars got in their whole body...."

"Really?" McQueen felt flush with pride. *The King sure knows quality racing when he sees it,* the rookie thought. "Oh, that, that's—"

"But you're stupid," The King finished.

McQueen blinked. "Excuse me?"

"This ain't a one-man deal, kid," The King said. "You need to wise up and get yourself a good crew chief and a good team. You ain't gonna win unless you got good folks behind you and you let them do their job like they should. It's like I tell the boys at the shop: it's about everybody comin' together and doin' the best they can."

"Uh, yeah, that is spectacular advice," McQueen said absently. He wasn't really paying attention to what The King was saying. He was too busy picturing himself as the next Dinoco car, his face on the cover of magazines, his signature on the side of the company helicopter, fame, fortune, and more Piston Cups than he could fit into his enormous mansion. And it was all starting right there, right then, with that win. "Thank you, Mr. The King."

Just then, music sounded over the PA system. "Ladies and gentlemen," Bob announced, "for the first time in Piston Cup history . . ."

". . . a rookie has won the Piston Cup!" McQueen shouted. "Yes!" Revving his engine, he drove forward, bursting through the victory banner. He struck his finish line pose, mugging for the crowd.

". . . we have a three-way tie!" Bob finished.

Confetti cannons burst, showering bits of paper through the air like snowflakes. The King and Chick drove forward to join McQueen.

"Oh, boy!" Chick said as he cracked up. "Hey, McQueen," he taunted, "that must be really embarrassing!"

McQueen scowled.

"Piston Cup officials have determined that a tiebreaker race between the three leaders will be held in California in one week," Bob announced.

McQueen was shocked. He couldn't believe that he hadn't won!

"Hey, rook," Chick whispered to McQueen, "first one to California gets Dinoco all to himself!"

McQueen slunk away, dejected. " 'First one to California gets Dinoco all to himself,' " he muttered. "Oh, we'll see who gets there first, Chick."

"**H**ey, kid!" Mack called as McQueen headed toward him. "Congrats on the tie!"

"I don't want to talk about it," the rookie replied grumpily. "C'mon, let's go, Mack. Saddle up. What'd you do with my trailer?"

"I parked it over at your sponsor's tent," Mack said. "You gotta make your personal appearance."

McQueen groaned. His sponsor was Rust-eze Medicated Bumper Ointment, and the tent was always filled with rusty old cars. McQueen would have preferred something flashier, like Dinoco, but it was Rust-eze that had given him his big break. And a contract was a contract. He had to make a personal appearance, and that was that. He forced a smile and drove into the tent.

"Nothing soothes a rusty bumper like Rust-eze,"

McQueen's recorded image said over a plasma TV screen in the back of the tent. "Wow, look at that shine! Use Rust-eze and you, too, can look like me. *Ka-chow!*"

The race car heaved a sigh as he watched his bosses—two brothers who were the owners of Rust-eze—tell their usual bad jokes. The rusty cars who filled the tent laughed their bumpers off at everything the two brothers said.

"I remember this car from Swampscott," one brother said to the crowd, "he was so rusty, he didn't even cast a shadow!"

The assembled cars hooted and honked as soon as they saw their hero.

"*Ecck* . . . I hate rusty cars," McQueen muttered under his breath. "This is *not* good for my image." He slunk behind a cardboard cutout of himself, trying to hide.

"Hey, look, there he is!" one of the brothers cried, catching sight of McQueen.

"Our almost champ!" the other shouted. "Get your rear end in here, kid!"

A spotlight flashed onto McQueen. He made his

way through the rusty cars, greeted the crowd, and forced himself to laugh at his bosses' jokes. Finally, it was time for him to go.

"Aw, we love you," his boss said as McQueen backed into his trailer, "and we're lookin' forward to another great year—just like this year!"

McQueen smiled. Then the gate crashed down. "Not on your life," he grumbled.

Mack hitched himself to the trailer, and soon he was hauling Lightning McQueen west. His face appeared on a video link inside Lightning's cabin.

"California, here we come!" Mack sang.

"Dinoco, here we come!" McQueen said to himself as he scanned the trophies and plaques that lined the walls and shelves of his trailer. He couldn't wait to land the glamorous new sponsor.

Just as McQueen had settled under the buffer for a massage, the phone rang.

"Is this the world's fastest racing machine?" asked a smooth voice at the other end of the line.

McQueen perked up at the sound of his agent's voice. "Is that you, Harv? Buddy!"

"Kid," Harv replied, "it is such an honor to be your agent that it almost hurts me to take ten percent of your winnings . . . and merchandising. And ancillary rights in perpetuity. Anyway, what a race, huh, champ? Didn't see it, but I heard you were great. Listen, they're giving you twenty tickets for the tiebreaker thing in Cali. I'll pass 'em on to your friends; you shoot me the names."

"Right. Friends." McQueen paused. Who was there to invite? The truth was, he had tons of fans . . . but he couldn't think of any real friends. He was speechless.

"Okay, I get it, Mr. Popular," Harv broke in. "So many friends you can't narrow it down."

McQueen didn't bother correcting him.

"Okay, gotta jump, kid," Harv said. "Let me know how it goes."

Harv hung up, and McQueen's eyes wandered to the window. A minivan weighted down with a mattress tied to its roof struggled to pass them.

Many long hours later, McQueen got more and more impatient. *Can't we go any faster?* he wondered. "Oh, come on, Mack," he complained over the intercom. "You're in the slow lane. This is Lightning McQueen you're hauling here."

Mack headed toward a truck stop. "Just stopping off for a quick breather, kid," he explained. "Ol' Mack needs a rest."

"Absolutely not!" McQueen insisted. "We're driving straight through all night until we get to California. We agreed to it."

Mack groaned. "All night? May I remind you, federal D.O.T. regs state—"

"C'mon, Mack." McQueen's voice softened. "I need to get there before Chick and hang with Dinoco." McQueen really wanted to move.

Mack looked at the truck stop, where a line of semis slept peacefully. "Hey, kid," Mack said gently, "I don't know if I can make it."

"Oh, sure you can, Mack!" McQueen said brightly. "Look, it'll be easy. I'll stay up with you! All night long."

Finally, Mack agreed to keep going down the dark Interstate.

McQueen kept Mack company for a short while, until he fell asleep. Mack traveled the endless miles alone. The lines dividing the lanes rolled like ribbons under his tires, and soon he felt his headlights drooping.

Mack was desperately trying to shake himself awake when a group of flashy hot rods rolled up beside him. Boost, the leader, noticed that Mack was falling asleep, and decided to have some fun. "We got ourselves a nodder," he told the other cars.

DJ, a car with enormous speakers, put on some soothing music.

"Pretty music," Mack said sleepily. He let out a huge yawn. In the next moment, he was snoring as he rolled forward.

"Yo, Wingo!" Boost called as he bumped Mack

toward his friend. "Lane change, man!"

"Right back at ya!" Wingo said as he booted Mack back across the highway. But Boost swerved out of the way, allowing Mack to bump onto the shoulder of the road.

"Oops, I missed," Boost said, and the hot rods cracked up.

Inside McQueen's trailer, the jostling caused a trophy to slip off the shelf. It hit the lift control button, and the back door fell open. McQueen rolled to the lip of the ramp as Mack, still fast asleep and moving forward, veered back onto the highway.

Suddenly, Snot Rod felt a sneeze coming on. *"Ahh . . . Ahh . . . Ahh . . . Ahh—"*

"He's gonna blow!" Wingo cried.

"Ah-chooo!" Snot Rod sneezed, sending a burst of flame from his tailpipe.

Mack swerved as he was startled awake. "Gesundheit!" he said automatically—then he realized where he was. "Whoa! One should never drive while drowsy." He didn't know that in the commotion McQueen had been shaken off the ramp! Mack kept driving into the night, leaving

McQueen alone on the highway.

Honk!

"Get out of the way!" cried a car as he sped around the sleeping McQueen—who had just rolled into oncoming traffic. "You're going the wrong way! Ahhhh!"

Cars honked and shouted as they veered to avoid McQueen.

"Mack!" McQueen hollered as he bolted awake, swerving just in time to avoid an oncoming truck.

Turning sharply, McQueen dodged through the traffic after his trailer, who still hadn't noticed that the race car was missing. But McQueen couldn't see where he was going. Race cars drove only on tracks—and the tracks were always lit up—so McQueen didn't have real headlights. "Mack!" he cried, momentarily losing sight of the truck. "Mack, wait for me!"

But Mack was too far ahead; he couldn't hear McQueen.

McQueen was gaining ground. He followed the truck's taillights as it headed to an off-ramp. Leaving the highway for a rural road, the trailer barreled over some train tracks. McQueen sped up—and jumped the crossing a millisecond before a train came through.

But when McQueen pulled up beside the truck, he made a horrible discovery. The trailer he'd been following wasn't Mack at all.

"Turn on your lights, you moron," the truck yelled at McQueen.

"Mack . . . ," McQueen whispered to himself as the truck drove away. So . . . if that truck wasn't Mack, where could Mack be? "The Interstate," McQueen said. Turning, he spotted some lights. He tore toward them at top speed, not realizing that he was headed down winding old Highway 66, not the Interstate.

A siren blasted through the night air, and McQueen saw red and blue flashing lights. A police car! "Maybe he can help me," McQueen said, slowing down.

But the police cruiser was old, and he hadn't had to chase a sleek young race car in years. *Ka-blam!* He backfired.

"He's shooting at me," McQueen said, panicking

and putting the pedal to the metal. "Why's he shooting at me?"

Boom! Boom! Ka-blam! "I haven't gone this fast in years," the Sheriff said to himself as he sped after McQueen. "I'm gonna blow a gasket!"

Thinking he was being gunned down, McQueen swerved, snakelike, to avoid the blasts.

"What in the blue blazes?" cried the Sheriff. "Crazy hot-rodder."

McQueen and the Sheriff barreled toward the sleepy little town of Radiator Springs. It was perfectly quiet there, and the locals were all gathered at Flo's V8 Café, looking up at the town's lone traffic light.

"I'm telling you, man," said Fillmore, an aging bus. "Every third blink is slower."

An old army jeep named Sarge gave Fillmore a dubious look. "The sixties weren't good to you, were they?"

Blam! Blam! Ka-blam!

Tires squealed and the siren wailed as McQueen tore toward town with the Sheriff right on his bumper. As McQueen approached the traffic light, he got his first real look at Radiator Springs.

"What?" the race car cried. "That's not the Interstate! Ow!" He slammed into a bunch of traffic cones. "Ow! Ow! Ow!" McQueen swerved to avoid the cones and found himself headed straight for a barbed wire fence! "No-no-no-no-no!" He burst through the fence, and the wire wrapped around him. He dragged the fence forward as he plowed past the café.

"I'm not the only one seeing this, right?" Fillmore asked as he stared at the out-of-control race car in disbelief.

McQueen fishtailed, hitting a bunch of oilcans and a stack of tires. Then he ground the garden of Red, the fire truck, into the dirt. He swerved to avoid the statue of the town's founder, Stanley, but the barbed wire caught it. For a moment, McQueen was pinned, spinning his wheels in place against the weight of the heavy statue, but then he gunned the engine. The statue tipped forward, landing in front of McQueen.

"Ahhh!" McQueen screamed, driving away, dragging Stanley and the barbed wire fence behind him and ripping up the road. Veering to the side, the

statue launched off a flatbed trailer like a water-skier and landed in some telephone wires. McQueen tried to get free, but he was still tangled in the barbed wire with Stanley. Suddenly, Stanley flew backward, as if flung from a giant slingshot.

"Fly away, Stanley," Fillmore called as the statue sailed overhead. "Be free."

The statue landed back on its pedestal, and McQueen got tangled even more in a set of low-hanging telephone wires.

The winded sheriff drove up to McQueen, who was hanging upside down by the poles. "Boy," the Sheriff said, catching his breath. "You're in a heap of trouble."

With a sigh, McQueen's engine sputtered to a stop. He had passed out.

When McQueen opened his eyes the next morning, he could hardly make out the blurry shape in front of him.

"Oh, boy . . . ," McQueen said groggily. "Where am I? What—?"

McQueen squinted. It took him a moment to figure out what he was looking at: a rusty old tow truck staring at him through a chain-link fence.

"Morning, Sleepin' Beauty!" the tow truck sang.

"Aha! Boy, I was wonderin' when you was gonna wake up!"

"Ahh!" McQueen cried, startled. "T-t-take whatever you want! Just don't hurt me!" He gunned his engine, but he didn't move. He looked down at his tire. "A parking boot?" he cried in horror at the metal clamp that pinned him in place. "Why do I

have a parking boot on? What do you— What's going on here, please?"

The tow truck burst into a gap-toothed grin. "You're funny," he said. "I like you already! My name's Mater!"

McQueen was so surprised by the strange name that he stopped struggling against his parking boot. "Mater?"

"Yeah, like 'tuh-mater,'" the tow truck explained, "but without the 'tuh.' What's your name?"

"What?" McQueen asked. "Look, I need to get to California as fast as possible. Where am I?"

"Where are ya?" Mater asked. "Shoot. You're in Radiator Springs, the cutest little town in Carburetor County."

McQueen looked around. All he could see was a dreary row of boarded-up buildings. It didn't look so cute to him. "Oh, great," he said sarcastically. "Just great!"

"Well, if you think that's great," Mater said proudly, "you should see the rest of the town!"

McQueen was starting to realize that Mater

wasn't the fastest car on the racetrack, which gave him an idea. "You know," McQueen said craftily, "I'd love to see the rest of the town, so if you could just open the gate, take this boot off, you and me — we go cruisin', check out the local scene, you know?"

"Dadgum!" Mater cried. "Cool!" He started to open the gate when a shout stopped him in his tracks.

"Mater!" bellowed the Sheriff as he rolled up. "What did I tell you about talking to the accused?"

Mater looked sheepish. "To not to."

"Well, quit your yappin'," the Sheriff snarled, "and tow this delinquent road hazard to traffic court."

"The Radiator Springs Traffic Court will come to order!" the Sheriff called as McQueen rolled into the front of the courtroom, his boot clomping.

The townsfolk were gathered in the courtroom—and they were not happy.

"Hey," called Ramone, a lowrider with a flashy paint job. "You scratched my paint. I ought to take a blowtorch to you, man!"

"Did you see what he did to my Stanley?" cried Lizzie, the oldest resident of the town.

A glamorous show car frowned at McQueen, indignant. "You see what he did to my café?" Flo demanded. "Now I've gotta restack the cans."

"You broke the road," scolded the small Italian import named Luigi. He owned Luigi's Casa Della Tires—and the tires McQueen had plowed through the night before. "You're a very bad car."

"Fascist!" Fillmore called.

"Commie!" bellowed Sarge.

"Officer, talk to me, babe," McQueen said to the Sheriff in a smooth voice. "How long is this gonna take? I gotta get to California, pronto."

"Where's your lawyer?" the Sheriff demanded.

"I don't know," McQueen admitted. "Tahiti, maybe?"

"When a defendant has no lawyer, the court will assign one to him. Hey!" the Sheriff called out to the assembled cars. "Anyone want to be his lawyer?"

"Shoot," Mater said. "I'll do it, Sheriff!"

McQueen groaned.

"All rise," Sheriff called. "The Honorable Doc Hudson presiding! May Doc have mercy on your soul."

An old blue car rolled into court and took his place at the judge's bench. "All right," Doc ranted, "I want to know who's responsible for wrecking my town, Sheriff. I want his hood on a platter. I'm going to put him in jail till he rots—no, check that. I'm gonna put him in jail till the jail rots on top of him

31

and then I'm going to move him to a new jail and let that one rot. I'm—" Doc stopped short, narrowing his eyes as he got a good look at McQueen.

The race car laughed nervously.

"Throw him out of here, Sheriff," Doc said in an official voice. "I want him out of my courtroom. I want him out of our town. Case dismissed!"

"Yes!" McQueen cried as the townsfolk gasped.

"Boy," Mater said to himself. "I'm pretty good at this lawyering stuff."

Just then, a sleek blue sports car drove into the courtroom. "Sorry I'm late, Your Honor," she said.

"Holy Porsche," McQueen muttered, awestruck by the gorgeous car. "She's gotta be from my attorney's office. Hey, thanks for coming," he said suavely, "but we're all set. He's letting me go."

"He's letting you go?" she repeated.

"Yeah, your job's pretty easy today." McQueen grinned. "All you have to do now is stand there and let me look at you. Listen, I'm going to cut to the chase. Me. You. Dinner." He flashed his lightning bolt sticker. *"Ka-chow!"*

"Ow!" the blue sports car cried as the reflected

light shone in her pretty eyes.

"I know," McQueen growled, moving in close to her. "I get that reaction a lot." He revved his engine.

"Okay . . . ," she said, unimpressed. She excused herself to talk to the judge.

"Do what you gotta do, baby," McQueen told her. "Oh, but listen, be careful. Folks around here are not firing on all cylinders, if you know what I mean."

"I'll keep that in mind," the blue sports car replied as she rolled forward. "Hey there, Mater," she added as she drove past the tow truck.

"Howdy, Sally," Mater replied.

McQueen gaped. "You know her?"

"She's the town attorney," Mater explained. "And my fiancée."

"What?" McQueen cried.

"*Naah,* just kiddin'," Mater said, giving McQueen a friendly nudge. "She just likes me for my body."

"Doc, you really look great this morning," Sally gushed to the judge. "Did you do something different with your side-view mirrors?"

Doc Hudson sighed. "What do you want, Sally?"

"Come on," she pleaded, "make this guy fix the road. The town needs this." Sally not only acted as the town attorney, she also owned the Cozy Cone Motel. She knew that the town was dependent on the road. How would they ever get customers if no one could drive to Radiator Springs?

Doc shot McQueen an angry glance. "No. I know his type. Race car." His grill tucked into a frown. "He's the last thing this town needs."

"Fellow citizens," Sally said, turning to the cars who lined the courtroom, "you're all aware of our town's proud history. It is our job and our pleasure to take care of the travelers on our stretch of that road. How, I ask you, are we to care for travelers if there is no road for them to drive on? Luigi, what do you have at your store?"

"Tires," the little Italian import replied.

"And if no one can get to you?" Sally prompted.

"I won't sell any tires," Luigi replied. His front bumper dropped in horror. "I will lose everything!"

"Flo, what'll happen if no one can come to your station to buy gas?" Sally asked the café owner.

"I'll go out of business and we'll have to leave town!" Flo cried.

Sally turned to the revved-up crowd. "And what's going to happen to all of us if Flo leaves town and closes her station?"

Suddenly, the entire town realized that their very lives depended on that road!

"So don't you think the car responsible should fix our road?" Sally demanded. "Oh, he can do it," she said, casting a look in McQueen's direction. "He's got the horsepower. So what do you want him to do?"

"Fix the road!" the cars shouted, rallying.

"Because we are a town worth fixing!" Sally was on a roll now.

"Order in the court!" Doc shouted. Once the courtroom was quiet, the irritated judge gave Sally a sidelong glance.

"Seems like my mind has been changed for me," Doc finally said grudgingly.

McQueen was furious. "Oh, I am so not taking you to dinner," he grumbled to Sally.

"Oh, that's okay, *Stickers*." Sally smiled, poking

fun at his sticker-covered frame. "You can take Bessie."

"Bessie," McQueen repeated. "Who's Bessie?"

"This here is Bessie," Doc said as he showed McQueen the massive piece of heavy machinery. She was steaming and dripping, and she was covered by a thick layer of tar. "Finest road-pavin' machine ever built," Doc announced. "I'm hereby sentencing you to community service. You're gonna fix the road under my supervision."

"What?" McQueen demanded, completely repulsed. "This place is crazy."

"Hey," Mater whispered, leaning in close to McQueen. "I know this might be a bad time right now, but you owe me thirty-two thousand dollars in legal fees."

"What?" McQueen cried.

"So we're gonna hitch you up to sweet Bessie," Doc went on, "and you're gonna pull her nice."

"You gotta be kidding me!" McQueen complained. He couldn't believe it. Did this old lemon seriously expect a flashy race car like Lightning McQueen to haul around a tub of junk like Bessie? As far as punishment went, this was cruel and unusual. "How long is this gonna take?"

"Well," Doc said thoughtfully, "if a fella does it right, should take him about five days."

"Five days?" McQueen cried. An image of Chick chatting up the folks at Dinoco flashed through his mind. "But I should be in California schmoozing Dinoco right now!"

"Then if I were you," Doc shot back, "I'd quit yappin' and start workin'. Hook him up, Mater."

"Okey-dokey." The tow truck rolled forward to attach McQueen to Bessie. But the minute he removed McQueen's parking boot—*zoom!*

"Freedom!" McQueen shouted loudly as he zipped away. "Woo-hoo! California, here I come!" He pressed the accelerator, shooting toward the WELCOME TO RADIATOR SPRINGS billboard. But suddenly, he coughed. Then he sputtered. "No. No, no, no," McQueen cried as he slowed to a stop. "Out of gas? How can I be out of gas?"

"Boy," Sheriff said as he and Sally rolled out from behind the billboard, "we ain't as dumb as you think we are."

"We siphoned your gas while you were passed out," Sally added. She could hardly hide her grin. *"Ka-chow!"*

Sheriff joined Sarge and Fillmore, who were having a quart of oil at Flo's and watching McQueen haul Bessie over the road. Red was tending to some flowers near the tire shop while Luigi fiddled with his tire tower.

"Red, can you move over?" old Lizzie croaked from the porch of her souvenir shop. "I want to get a look at that sexy hot rod!"

"You know, I used to be a pretty good whistler," Mater said to McQueen as the rookie race car struggled to haul Bessie. McQueen inched along, gagging on fumes from the tar. "I can't do it now, of course," Mater went on, "on account of sometimes I get fluid built up in my engine block, but Doc said he's gonna fix it, though. He can fix about anything. That's why we made him the judge. Boy, you shoulda heard me on the song 'Giddy Up Oom Papa Mow-Mow.' Now, I'm not one to brag, but people come pretty far to see me get low on the 'mow-mow.'"

Bessie let out a squirt of tar. It landed all over McQueen's lightning bolt sticker.

"Aw, man, that's just great. My lucky sticker's all dirty," McQueen griped. "Hey!" he called to the fire truck.

Red looked up from his flowers.

"Yeah, you in the red!" McQueen went on. "I could use a little hose down. Help me wash this off."

Red darted into the firehouse garage.

"Where's he going?" McQueen asked.

"Oh, he's just a little bit shy," Mater explained. "And he hates you for killing his flowers."

"I shouldn't have to put up with this," McQueen grumbled angrily. "I am a precision instrument of speed and aerodynamics."

Mater looked blank. "You hurt your what?"

"I'm a very famous race car!" McQueen shouted.

"You are a famous race car?" Luigi cried, brightening. "I must scream to the world my excitement from the top of someplace very high! Do you know many Ferraris?"

"No," McQueen admitted. "They race on the European circuit. I'm in the Piston Cup—"

The little Italian import was unimpressed. "Luigi follow only the Ferraris," he interrupted. Then he drove off, leaving McQueen still strapped to Bessie.

Just then, two minivans appeared on the horizon, heading into town.

"Customers, everyone!" Sally cried. "It's been a long time; just remember what we rehearsed. You all know what to do."

The town sprang into action, taking their places in front of their shops and flipping over their OPEN signs.

"I just don't see any on-ramp anywhere," Mrs. Mini Van pointed out. She and her husband bumped awkwardly over the broken road. They were looking for the Interstate.

"I know exactly where we are," Mr. Mini Van

insisted, even though he didn't.

"Hello!" Sally chirped as she raced to welcome the motorists. "Welcome to Radiator Springs, gateway to Ornament Valley, legendary for its quality service and friendly hospitality. How can we help you?"

"We don't need anything," Mr. Mini Van said, "thank you very much."

"Oh, honey, ask for directions to the Interstate," Mrs. Mini Van begged. Her husband ignored her.

"What you really need is the sweet taste of my homemade organic fuel," Fillmore suggested.

"We're just trying to find the Interstate," Mrs. Mini Van explained.

"Good to see you, soldier," barked the old jeep. "Come on by Sarge's Surplus Hut."

"I do have a map over at the Cozy Cone Motel," Sally told the couple helpfully. "And if you do stay, we offer a free Lincoln Continental breakfast."

"I don't need a map," Mr. Mini Van said stubbornly. "I have the GPS."

Flo offered them fuel. Luigi suggested that they get some new tires. Ramone even tried to sell the lost couple a flashy new paint job.

But the travelers weren't interested. In fact, all the attention made them drive a little faster to get out of Radiator Springs.

"Come back soon, okay?" Sally called as the couple sped off. "I mean, you know where we are. Tell your friends."

"*Pssst. Pssst.*" McQueen gestured to the couple as they neared the edge of town. "Hey—I know how to get to the Interstate."

"Oh, do you?" Mrs. Mini Van asked as she came to a stop.

"No," McQueen admitted, "not really, but listen. I'm Lightning McQueen, the famous race car. I'm being held here against my will and I need you to call my team so they can come rescue me and get me to California in time for me to win the Piston Cup!"

The Mini Vans exchanged nervous glances. This car sounded crazy.

"Gotta be goin' now," Mr. Mini Van said quickly. "Okay, bye-bye!"

Now McQueen was desperate.

"No, no, no!" McQueen begged. Now he really

sounded insane. But what else could he do? He didn't care if he sounded out of his mind. The thought of staying in Radiator Springs was making him crazy!

He yelled after the Mini Vans, "It's the truth! I'm telling you, you gotta help me!"

But the Mini Vans took off without checking their rearview mirrors.

"And we'll be right back to our Hank Williams marathon after a quick Piston Cup update," a voice announced over the radio on Lizzie's porch.

McQueen looked up. Piston Cup update? Had anyone even noticed he was gone yet? He wondered. Maybe they'd send a search party!

"Still no sign of Lightning McQueen," the announcer said.

McQueen's engine raced. They *were* looking for him! Maybe that minivan couple would tell someone they had seen him.

"Meanwhile, Chick Hicks arrived in California and today became the first car to spend practice time on the track," the voice went on.

"Yeah, well, it's just nice to get out here before the other competitors," Chick's voice boomed over the radio's speakers. "You know, get a head start."

McQueen glowered, imagining Chick and Tex laughing together at the Dinoco tent. He imagined Chick winning the Piston Cup, getting the big endorsement deals, starring in a Hollywood movie— getting everything McQueen wanted for himself.

Well, this race car isn't about to quit now, McQueen thought, snapping out of his vision. "Mater," he said to the rusty old tow truck, "let me get this straight. I can go when this road is done. That's the deal, right?"

"That's what they done did said," Mater agreed.

That was all McQueen needed to hear. "Okay. Out of my way," he growled. "I've got a road to finish." McQueen focused, the way he did before a race. Then, in a moment, he was off! He put the hammer down and zipped through his work. Bessie wobbled and splashed tar across the road, groaning as the race car pulled her far faster than she was built to go.

A short while later, Mater burst into Doc's office. "He's done!"

"Done?" Doc grumbled. He wasn't sure whether

to be impressed or suspicious. "It's only been an hour." He followed Mater out toward the street, where the rest of the town was gathered. They looked at their newly "fixed" road. It was a disaster.

"I'm done." McQueen panted heavily. "Look, I'm finished. Just say thank you," he said to Sally, "and I'll be on my way. That's all you gotta say."

"Whee-hoo!" Mater called as he drove to the opposite end of the road. "I'm the first one on the new road!" He drove over the bumpy splattered asphalt. "A-h-h-a-h!" he said as he was jostled back and forth. "It rides pre-etty smo-ooo-ooth."

Sally cut to the chase. "It looks awful."

McQueen glared at her. "Now it matches the rest of the town," he shot back.

Red, the shy fire truck, was so hurt by McQueen's comment that he drove off into the woods, knocking over Luigi's tower of tires. The whole town could hear Red sobbing.

Furious, Sally wheeled to face McQueen. "Who do you think you are?" she demanded.

"Look, Doc said when I finished, I could go," McQueen said in frustration. "That was the deal."

"The deal was you fix the road, not make it worse," Doc snapped as he drove up. "Now, scrape it off; start over again."

"Hey, look, grandpa," McQueen said rudely. "I'm not a bulldozer, I'm a race car."

"Is that right?" Doc replied, clearly unimpressed. "Then why don't we just have a little race? Me and you."

McQueen cracked up. "Ho, ho, ho. Me and you," he said, unbelieving. "Is that a joke?"

"If you win, you go and I fix the road," Doc suggested. "If I win, you do the road *my* way."

McQueen couldn't believe his luck! *This car probably does zero to sixty in about three-point-five years,* he thought. *I'll run the race and be out of here in half an hour.* It was an offer he couldn't refuse.

"You know what, old-timer?" McQueen said. "That's a wonderful idea. Let's race."

"**G**entlemen, this will be a one-lap race," Sheriff announced as the whole town assembled at Willys Butte to watch the action. "You will drive to Willys Butte, go around Willys Butte, and come back. There will be no bumpin', no cheatin', no spittin', no bitin', no road rage, no maimin', no oil slickin', no pushin', no shovin', no backstabbin', no road-hoggin', and no lollygaggin'."

McQueen was hardly listening. "Speed," he said to himself. "I am speed."

"Gentlemen," announced Sheriff, "start your engines."

Doc's engine turned over slowly, coughing and sputtering. With a smug laugh, McQueen started his own engine. It roared dangerously.

"Great idea, Doc," Sally muttered to herself.

"Now the road will never get done."

Luigi dropped the flag, and McQueen took off like a rocket. The town cheered as he sent up a cloud of dust behind his rear tires. But when the dust cleared, everyone saw that Doc was still standing at the starting line!

"Doc, the flag means 'go,' " Luigi explained.

Doc didn't move.

"Uh, Doc?" Ramone said slowly. "What are you doing, man?"

"Oh, dear," Doc said in a flat voice. "It would seem I'm off to a poor start. Well, better late than never." He turned to the rusty tow truck. "Come on, Mater. You got your tow cable?"

"Well, yeah," Mater said as he and Doc rolled along the track, far behind McQueen. "I always got my tow cable. Why?"

"Oh," Doc said, "just in case."

Curious, the other cars followed Doc and Mater.

McQueen was flying along the road, showing off his incredible speed. "I am speed," he said to himself, taking the turn as he rounded the turn on the dirt track. "Nothing can stop me now.

I'm halfway to California—"

Whoa! The turn was tight, and before he could register what was happening, McQueen had lost control, dropping off a low cliff and landing hard in the sand below.

"Ooh, man!" Ramone said, wincing at the sight of McQueen. The race car was wedged in a grove of sharp cacti. "Ow!"

"Whoa . . . ," Fillmore agreed. "Bad trip, man."

McQueen revved his engine, but it was no use. He couldn't move.

Mater giggled.

"You drive like you fix roads . . . ," Doc said as McQueen spun his wheels. ". . . lousy." The judge turned to the tow truck. "Have fun fishing, Mater."

As Doc drove away, Mater cast down his towline and dragged McQueen up the hill by his rear axle. "I'm startin' to think he knowed you was gonna crash," Mater said to the race car.

"Thank you, Mater," McQueen said gratefully as the tow truck pulled him back onto the track.

Radiator Springs was turning out to be harder to leave than he'd ever expected.

"I can make a little turn on dirt, you think? No!" McQueen grumbled late that night as he scraped off the asphalt he had poured over the broken road. "And now I'm a day behind. I'm never gonna get out of here."

"Hey," Ramone called as McQueen muttered to himself, "you need a new paint job, man."

"No, thank you," McQueen said automatically. He didn't have time for a new paint job; he needed to fix that road! He couldn't believe he had lost a race to an old grandpa car!

"How about some organic fuel?" Fillmore suggested hopefully.

McQueen sighed. "Pass."

"Whoo!" Flo said, eyeing McQueen. "Watchin' him work is makin' me thirsty. Anybody else want something to drink?"

"Nah, not me, Flo," Mater said. "I'm on one of them there special diets. I'm a pre-sisional instrument of speed and aero-matics."

McQueen grumbled on. " 'You race like you fix roads . . . ,' " he mimicked, mocking Doc's insult. "I'll show him. I will show him." He grunted, throwing himself into his work. Soon he had finished the scraping. He hooked himself up to Bessie and started repaving.

Splat!

"Aww, great!" McQueen shouted as he tried to shake off the tar Bessie had squirted all over him. "I hate it, hate, hate, hate, hate it!"

But no matter how much he hated it, McQueen kept on working all through the night.

"Whee-hee!" Mater shouted the next morning as dawn broke over Radiator Springs. "Whee-hoo!"

Hearing the whoops and hollers, Sally drove out of her motel to investigate. She found Mater turning circles and spinning happily on a beautiful newly paved stretch of road. She gasped.

Wow, she thought. McQueen had done an amazing job!

"Morning, Sally," Mater called. "Hey, look at this here fancy new road that Lightning McQueen done just made!"

Soon the other cars had gathered on the road. Ramone bounced on his hydraulics, getting as low as he could go.

"Oooh, Ramone," Flo cooed to her husband, "Mama ain't seen you that low in years."

"I haven't seen a road like this in years," Ramone replied.

"Well, then," Flo said playfully, "let's cruise, baby."

Soon all the cars were out taking a spin on the sleek new blacktop.

"E bellissima!" Luigi cried as he gawked at the road from the front of his store. "It's like it was paved by angels!"

"Doc, look at this," Sally said as the gruff old roadster pulled up to the fresh asphalt. "Shoulda tossed him into the cactus a lot sooner, huh?"

Doc grunted. "Well, he ain't finished yet. He's still got a long way to go."

"Hey, Luigi!" Lizzie called as she rolled past the tire store. "This new road makes your place look like a dump!"

"Ah, the crazy old devil woman—" Luigi said grouchily. But as he looked up at his store, he gasped. "She's-a right!"

Doc peered down at the road, inspecting the work closely. "Huh—that punk actually did a good job," he muttered. "Well, now, where the heck is he?" Looking around, he noticed Bessie sitting by the side of the road. McQueen was nowhere in sight.

Just then, Doc heard the sound of a race car engine in the distance. He sped off after the noise.

"Sheriff," Doc said as he drove up to the cliff edge at Willys Butte, "is he making another run for it?"

Sheriff chuckled. "No, no," he explained, "he ran out of asphalt in the middle of the night and asked me if I could come down here. All he's trying to do is make that there turn."

Sure enough, McQueen was rounding the same turn that had made him wipe out the day before. Just as he reached it, his tires skidded, and he swerved, then crashed. "No, no, no, no!" McQueen cried as he drove back to try again. "Ahh, great! I've done perfect turns on every track I've ever raced on."

"Huh," Doc said as he watched McQueen try to make the curve over and over. He smiled a little at the race car's determination. "Sheriff, why don't you go get yourself a quart of oil at Flo's?" the judge suggested. "I'll keep an eye on him."

"Well, thanks, Doc," Sheriff said in surprise.

"I've been feelin' a quart low." He drove off, leaving Doc to deal with McQueen.

Doc watched carefully as McQueen tried the turn again. Sure enough, he wiped out, and he came to a stop, spitting dirt from his grill.

Finally, the old car decided to help out McQueen. "This ain't asphalt, son," Doc explained simply as he rolled up to the race car. "This is dirt."

"Oh, great," McQueen snapped. "So you're a judge, a doctor, and a racing expert?"

"I'll put it simple," Doc said patiently. "If you're going hard enough left, you'll find yourself turning right."

"Oh, right," McQueen said, his voice dripping with sarcasm. "That makes perfect sense. Turn right to go left. Thank you. Or should I say 'no, thank you,'" he went on, his voice rising in frustration, "because in Opposite World, maybe that really means thank you." *What does that old car know about racing, anyway?* McQueen thought as he took off on the track, throwing plumes of dust all over Doc.

Once the dust cleared, McQueen saw that Doc

had driven away. Suddenly, he began to wonder if Doc's advice might work. *Well, I might as well try it,* he thought. *Nothing else seems to be helping.*

McQueen sped toward the turn. "Turn right to go left," he said to himself. It didn't make any sense.

At the last moment, McQueen turned sharply right—and shot straight over the cliff.

"Ooh," he cried as he landed right back in the cacti. "Oh, that hurt."

"Turn right to go left," McQueen muttered later that afternoon as he pulled Bessie down the road. He was filthy and covered with cactus thorns. "Guess what? I tried it, and you know what? This crazy thing happened—I went right!"

"You keep talking to yourself, people'll think you're crazy," Lizzie said.

"Thanks for the tip," McQueen told the forgetful old car.

Lizzie glared at the race car. "I wasn't talking to you!"

Meanwhile, McQueen's gorgeous new road had inspired the townsfolk to spruce up their shops. Mater was using his cable to straighten his TOW MATER sign. Ramone was repainting a fence as Flo looked on, clearly impressed. Red was busy washing the leaning tower of tires.

"Che bellissimo!" Sally cried as she watched Luigi's assistant, Guido, paint the tire store while Luigi cleaned the windows. "It looks great!" She was thrilled to see the townspeople taking pride in Radiator Springs. *Actually,* she thought, *there's only one car who still needs a makeover. . . .* She looked over at the filthy race car, who was muttering to himself as he paved.

"While I'm stuck here paving this stinking road," he griped, "Chick's in California schmoozing Dinoco." McQueen pulled harder, working out his anger. "*My* Dinoco. Whoa, whoa, whoa!" he said, stopping to straighten up. "Who's touching me?"

"You have a slow leak," Luigi explained as Guido checked the air in McQueen's tires. Cactus prickles stuck out of the rubber like porcupine quills.

"Guido," Luigi said, motioning to his assistant, who held a can of tire sealant, "he fix. You make-a such-a nice new road. You come to my shop. Luigi take-a good care of you—even though you not a Ferrari. You buy four tires, I give you a full-size

The Dinoco 400 is the biggest race of the year. Lightning McQueen, Chick Hicks, and The King are the top contenders.

It's a three-way tie!

McQueen makes a mess in the little town
of Radiator Springs.

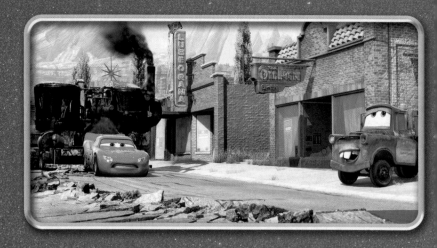

McQueen is sentenced to fixing the road
before he can leave the town.

McQueen works quickly. Everyone in town
thinks the new road is awful!

Doc challenges McQueen to a race.
The loser will fix the road.

McQueen loses to Doc.

The town wakes to a beautiful new stretch of road.

Inspired by the new road, everyone in town spruces up their shops.

Mater takes McQueen tractor tipping!

McQueen promises Mater a helicopter ride
if he wins his big race.

McQueen spends the night at the Cozy Cone.

McQueen discovers Doc's secret.

Sally shows McQueen what life is like
in the slow lane.

The folks from Radiator Springs
become McQueen's pit crew.

McQueen returns to Radiator Springs...
and he keeps his promise to Mater.

spare absolutely free." He smiled enthusiastically.

McQueen sighed. He was in a terrible mood. "Look," he said irritably, "I get all my tires for free." *Don't these people know anything about famous race cars?* he wondered.

Just as Luigi drove off, McQueen was blasted with cold water. "Ohh!" he screamed. "Stop!"

The water stopped, and McQueen found himself facing Red. Sally was standing beside him.

"Ooh, Red," Sally said, "you missed a spot. See it right there? Right on the hood? Right there."

"No, no—" McQueen cried as Red blasted the remaining piece of cactus on his hood. "Ah . . . stop!" he sputtered. "Ah, that's cold! Whoo! Help! Please! Stop!"

Red kept blasting water at McQueen until the cactus flew off.

"Thanks, Red," Sally said.

"What was that for?" McQueen demanded, coughing and blinking.

"Do you want to stay at the Cozy Cone, or what?" Sally asked bluntly. "I mean, if you do, you gotta be clean."

"What?" McQueen was really confused now. "I don't get it—"

"Nothing," Sally said, trying to sound as if it was no big deal. "I just thought I'd say thank you for doing a great job by letting you stay at the Cozy Cone."

McQueen was shocked. "Wait, you're being nice to me."

"I mean, if you want to stay at the dirty impound, that's fine," Sally went on. "You know, I understand—you criminal types."

"No, no, no, no—that's okay." McQueen looked in admiration at the motel in the distance. It was much nicer than the impound, that was for sure. "Yeah, the Cozy Cone."

"Cone number one, if you want." Sally drove off, accidentally running into a stack of orange cones. They tumbled all over. Embarrassed, she drove quickly into her motel office.

Just then, Mater appeared. He pulled up beside McQueen and began chattering away, "You know, I once knew this girl Doreen. Good-lookin' girl. Looked just like a Jaguar, only she was a truck. You know, I used to crash into her just so I could spoke to her." Mater grinned proudly.

"What are you talking about?" McQueen asked.

"I dunno," Mater admitted. "Hey, I know somethin' we can do tonight, 'cause I'm in charge of watchin' ya."

"No, Mater, I gotta finish this road and I have to get out of here."

"Well, that's all right, Mr. I-Can't-Turn-on-Dirt." Mater started to drive off. "You probably couldn't handle it, anyway."

"Whoa, whoa, easy now, Mater," McQueen said indignantly. "You know who you're talking to? This is Lightning McQueen. I can handle anything."

Later that night, McQueen found himself looking out at a herd of sleeping tractors. "Mater," he said, "I'm not doing this."

"Oh, c'mon," Mater urged, "you'll love it! Tractor tipping's fun! When I say go, we go. But don't let Frank catch you. Go!" Mater took off.

"Whoa!" McQueen cried. "Wha-who-who-who's Frank?" He peeled off after the tow truck. "Mater. Wait, Mater!"

"'Kay, here's what you do," Mater explained as he arrived at the bottom of the hill where the tractors stood sleeping. "You just sneak up in front of 'em and then honk, and they do the rest. Watch this." Slowly and quietly, Mater drove up to a tractor.

Honk!

The tractor startled awake. It let out a low moan

as it very slowly started tipping over. A puff of smoke burst from its exhaust pipe.

Mater cracked up. "I swear, tractors are so dumb!" he cried gleefully. He snuck up on another one and honked, then laughed as it tipped over. "I don't care who you are, that's funny right there. Oh, your turn, bud!"

"Mater, I can't," McQueen said. "I don't even have a horn."

"Baby!" Mater teased. Then he started imitating a chicken. "Bwak, bock, bock, bock!"

"Fine, stop, stop, okay?" McQueen sighed. "All right. I'll do something." He drove up to a sleeping tractor and revved his engine.

The roar was so loud that the whole field of tractors startled awake. With a group moan, they all tipped over.

McQueen and Mater laughed.

Suddenly, there was a strange whine, and in a moment, a giant tractor combine appeared. Blades whirling, he lunged at them like an angry bull.

"That's Frank!" Mater shouted, whipping around.

McQueen took off after the tow truck.

"Run! Run!" Mater hollered, laughing his bumper off. "Old Frank's gonna catch you! Run! He's gonna get you!"

McQueen didn't know why Mater was laughing; that combine was big and angry! Frank closed in behind as they tore toward an opening in the fence. They made it through the hole just in time and raced onto the open road as fast as their wheels could carry them.

"I haven't seen Frank that excited about somethin' since the last time he was excited about somethin'," Mater said as he and McQueen made their way back to town. "Must've been your red bumper. Tomorrow night we can go and look for the ghost light."

"I can't wait, Mater," McQueen said sarcastically.

"Oh, boy, you gotta admit that was fu-un," Mater said happily. "Well, we better get you back to the impound lot."

"Um, you know," McQueen said awkwardly, "actually, Sally's gonna let me stay at the motel."

"Oh . . . getting cozy at the Cone, is we?" Mater teased, arriving at the motel's parking lot.

"You're in love with Miss Sally."

"No, I'm not," McQueen said. "No way."

"*Way*. You're in love with Miss Sally." Mater turned his teasing into a singsong. "You're in love with Miss Sally." The tow truck turned around and started driving backward, taunting the race car. "You love 'er, you love 'er, you love 'er, you love 'er—"

"Will you stop that?" McQueen said.

"Stop what?" Mater asked.

"That driving backwards stuff," McQueen said with a shudder. "It's creepin' me out. You're going to wreck or something."

"Wreck? Shoot, I'm the world's best backwards driver. You just watch this right here, lover boy." With a whoop, Mater peeled out backward and wove between the Cozy Cone's traffic cone guest rooms. He cut close to them but didn't knock over a single one.

"What are you doing?" McQueen shouted as Mater swerved back and forth. "Watch out! Look out! Mater, stop showing off now, okay? Hey, take it easy, Mater! Look out!"

Mater hooted as he drove off between a few trees

and shrubs. "Ain't no need to watch where I'm going," he bragged as he headed toward McQueen at top speed. Just as he and McQueen were about to collide, Mater spun around and came to a full stop, facing the shocked race car. "Just need to know where I been!"

"Whoa!" McQueen said, truly impressed. "That was incredible." He laughed out loud. "How'd you do that?"

"Rearview mirrors," Mater said simply. "We'll get you some, and I'll teach you if you want."

"Yeah," McQueen said thoughtfully, "maybe I'll use it in my big race."

"What's so important about this race of yours, anyway?" Mater asked.

"It's not just a race." McQueen suddenly became serious as he explained. "We're talking about the Piston Cup. I've been dreaming about it my whole life. I'll be the first rookie in history ever to win it, and when I do, we're talking big new sponsor with private helicopters; no more medicated bumper ointment, no more rusty old cars—"

"What's wrong with rusty old cars?" Mater

asked, sounding hurt. After all, he himself was rusty and old.

"Well, I don't mean you, Mater," McQueen said, realizing his mistake. He hadn't meant to hurt Mater's feelings. "I mean *other* old cars. You know, not like you. I like you."

"It's okay, buddy," Mater said. "Hey, you think maybe one day I could get a ride in one of them helicopters? I mean, I've always wanted to ride in one of them fancy helicopters."

"Yeah, yeah," McQueen said casually. "Yeah, sure, sure."

"You mean it?" Mater's engine hummed in excitement.

"Oh, yeah," McQueen promised. "Anything you say."

Mater's smile disappeared, and his expression turned serious. "I knew it! I knowed I made a good choice."

"In what?" McQueen asked.

"My best friend," Mater said simply. McQueen smiled. Then Mater spun his tow cable like a helicopter propeller and sped away backward, flashing his one good headlight. "See you tomorrow, buddy!" he called. "McQueen and Sally, parked beneath a tree, k-i-s-sumpin', sumpin', sumpin' . . . t," he sang as he drove away.

McQueen couldn't help laughing as Mater's voice faded into the distance. Finally, he turned and started looking for his cone.

"Number one . . . ," he muttered as he searched. "Number one . . . " He found it. The race car drove inside and looked around. "Ah, this is nice—"

"Hey, Stickers!" Sally said, appearing outside the cone. "I overheard you talking to Mater."

McQueen was horrified. Had she overheard Mater teasing him about having a crush on her? He hoped not.

"When? You just—just now? What did—what did you hear?" he asked nervously.

"Oh, just something about a helicopter ride," Sally said.

"Oh, yeah, yeah," McQueen said, half to himself. "He got a kick out of that, didn't he?"

"Did you mean it?" Sally asked. "You'll get him a ride?"

"Oh," McQueen said absently. "Who knows? I mean, first things first. I gotta get outta here and make the race."

"You know," Sally said, "Mater trusts you."

McQueen thought about that for a moment. He hadn't really taken his promise to Mater seriously, but Mater *would* take it seriously. "Yeah, okay."

"Did you mean that?" Sally pressed.

"Look, I'm exhausted," McQueen said, not knowing what else to say. Then he added, "It's kinda been a long day."

"Yeah, okay," Sally said. "Night."

"Hey," McQueen called as she started to drive away. "You know, thanks for letting me stay here. It's nice to be out of the impound. And this is . . . it's great. Newly refurbished, right?"

Sally smiled. "Yeah." She was proud of her motel—and McQueen had just given her a real compliment. *Maybe there's some good in him after all,* she thought. "Good night."

McQueen moaned. He was having a terrible nightmare. It was the Piston Cup final, and he was being beaten—by Frank the combine! In a whirlwind, Frank took the trophy and the Dinoco sponsorship and had gorgeous female cars fawning all over him. It was horrible.

"No!" McQueen cried, startling awake. He looked at the alarm clock. A tiny car had just popped out of a cone and honked its horn. "I gotta get out of here."

McQueen sped off to find Sheriff. He needed his daily gas ration. But Sheriff wasn't at the impound, so McQueen zipped over to Doc Hudson's office.

"Hey, have you seen Sheriff?" McQueen asked as he burst into the office. He realized with a sudden start that Sheriff was up on a hydraulic lift, getting a private smog check. His entire underside was exposed! *"Ahh!"* McQueen cried in horror. "Oh my gosh."

"Hey, what are you doin'?" Doc Hudson demanded. "Wait for him at Flo's. Now, get out of here."

"I've been trying to get out of here for three days!" McQueen shot back.

"Hope you enjoyed the show!" Sheriff called as McQueen drove off.

On his way out, the frustrated race car kicked an old oilcan into Doc's garage. He cringed as something crashed inside. *Oops.* He hadn't meant to break anything. In spite of the signs that read NO TRESPASSING and PRIVATE PROPERTY, McQueen decided he'd better go inside and make sure everything was okay.

"Whoa, Doc," McQueen said as he drove cautiously into the office, "time to clean out the garage, buddy." He scanned the junk littering the garage; the place was piled high with mess. As he headed toward the back, he spotted something on Doc's desk. It was covered in dirt and filled with tools, but the shape was familiar. McQueen rolled over for a better look. He gasped at what he saw. It was a racing trophy. But not just any trophy—it was the Piston Cup!

THE HUDSON HORNET, it read, CHAMPION: 1951.

"He has a Piston Cup?" McQueen whispered, stunned. On the floor nearby were two more, from 1952 and 1953. "Oh my gosh, *three* Piston Cups?" He couldn't believe it. But sure enough, he came across a newspaper article proclaiming Doc "Champion for All Time."

"The sign says 'stay out,'" Doc growled as he appeared in the doorway.

"Y-you have three Piston Cups!" McQueen stammered. "You're the Hudson Hornet!"

"Wait over at Flo's," Doc snapped angrily, "like I told you."

McQueen started to leave, but in the doorway, he stopped in his tracks. "Of course!" he said, realizing the truth. "I-I can't believe I didn't see it before. You're the Fabulous Hudson Hornet. You still hold the record for most wins in a single season. Oh, we gotta talk. You gotta show me your tricks, please—"

"I already tried that," Doc pointed out.

"I mean, you won the championship three times!" McQueen gushed. "Look at those trophies!" .

"You look." Doc fixed McQueen with a steady gaze. "All I see is a bunch of empty cups." With that, he slammed the door in McQueen's face.

McQueen just couldn't keep news like that to himself. He knew that most of the townsfolk would be gathered at the café, so he zipped over there at top speed. "Oh my gosh!" he said as he drove into Flo's. "Guys! Did you know Doc is a famous race car?"

For a moment, everyone was silent.

Then they burst out laughing.

"Doc?" Sheriff cried. "Our Doc?"

"Not Doc Hudson?" Sarge bellowed.

"Did you hear that one?" Ramone—radiant in new yellow paint—was laughing hysterically. "He's saying Doc's a—this guy cracks me up!"

"No, no, no," McQueen insisted. He felt almost desperate. He had to convince them of who Doc was. "It's true! He's a real racing legend. He's the

Fabulous Hudson Hornet!"

"Fabulous?" Flo said doubtfully. "I've never seen Doc drive more than twenty miles an hour. I mean, have you ever seen him race?"

"No," McQueen admitted, "but I wish I could've." McQueen was dead serious. "They say he was amazing. He won three Piston Cups!"

Mater spat out the oil he'd been drinking. "He did what in his cup?"

McQueen tried to persuade them that Doc Hudson was the real deal, but the townsfolk didn't buy it.

"I think the heat's startin' to get to the boy," Sheriff said.

"Are you sick, buddy?" Mater asked.

Sally hit the gas lever with her tire. *Ding ding ding!* She filled up McQueen's tank.

"Hey! Hey!" Sheriff protested. This could be dangerous. "What're you doing?"

"It's okay, Sheriff," Sally said. "You can trust me, right?"

"I trust you, all right," Sheriff said, narrowing his eyes at McQueen. "It's him I'm worried about."

"I trust him," Sally said. "C'mon," she told McQueen. "Let's take a drive."

Once his tank was full, McQueen considered taking off for the open road. Nothing was stopping him now.

Sally started toward a mountain in the distance. "Hey, Stickers," she called. "You comin' or what?" She drove away, letting McQueen decide for himself whether to make a run for it.

After hesitating for just a moment, he took off after Sally.

"Mmm-hmm," Flo said knowingly to Sheriff. "And you thought he was gonna run."

"Okay," McQueen said as he caught up to Sally, "you got me out here. Where are we going?"

"I don't know." Sally zipped off.

McQueen was surprised by how fast Sally was as he chased her into a forest. Playfully, she splashed him with an icy puddle, and the shock took his breath away. Grinning, Sally tried to splash him again, but McQueen dodged the water—and ran into a puddle of mud.

Sally laughed as McQueen took off after her. He accidentally drove into a pile of leaves, which stuck to his muddy surface.

As they rounded a few turns, McQueen took the lead, but Sally shot past him again. The two cars passed through a rock tunnel as the road wound up the mountain. McQueen was starting to notice the natural beauty that surrounded him.

As he took a curve, McQueen caught sight of Sally passing a majestic waterfall up ahead. He was stunned by how beautiful she looked. He smiled at her and she laughed. His grill was covered in bugs!

McQueen spit the bugs out and took off after her again, and soon he found himself at the top of the mountain. Sally was stopped in front of an old abandoned motel.

"Wow," McQueen said as he looked around at the dusty motel. "What is this place?"

Sally sighed. "Wheel Well. Used to be the most popular stop on the Mother Road." She was referring to the old Highway 66.

McQueen looked carefully at Sally and wondered. She was a brand-new Porsche. A fancy car. Why was she living in the little town of Radiator Springs in the middle of nowhere?

"How does a Porsche wind up in a place like this?" he asked, marveling.

"Well, it's really pretty simple," Sally told him. "I was an attorney in L.A., living life in the fast lane. And you know what? It never felt . . . happy."

"Yeah . . . ," McQueen said thoughtfully, then caught himself. "I mean, really?"

"Yeah." Sally went on. "So I left California— just drove and drove and finally broke down right here. Doc fixed me up. Flo took me in. Well, they all did. And I never left."

McQueen thought for a moment. He had to admit, his time in Radiator Springs hadn't been all bad. Still, he couldn't really imagine himself living there. "I understand you need to recharge the old batteries, but you know, after a while, why didn't you go back?"

"I fell in love," Sally said simply.

McQueen's tires deflated a little. "Corvette?"

"No." Sally drove to the edge of the cliff. "I fell in love . . . with this."

McQueen followed her and looked down. "Whoa." Below them, Radiator Springs was a glistening green oasis at the base of a towering mountain range. The setting sun made the breathtaking waterfall sparkle in the distance. Beyond Radiator Springs, cars zipped by on the Interstate, oblivious to the beautiful scene. "Look at that," McQueen said to himself. "They're driving right by. They don't even know what they're missing."

"Forty years ago," Sally said, "that Interstate down there didn't exist. Back then, cars came across the country a whole different way."

"How do you mean?" McQueen asked.

"Well, the road didn't cut through the land like that Interstate," Sally explained. "It moved with the land; you know it rose, it fell, it curved. Cars didn't drive on it to make great time. They drove on it to *have* a great time."

McQueen was quiet. His whole life was about speed. The idea of driving slowly, for fun, was strange. "What happened?"

"The town got bypassed just to save ten minutes of driving," Sally said.

McQueen imagined what the Wheel Well and Radiator Springs must have been like when they were thriving. "How great would it have been to see this place in its heyday?"

"Oh," Sally said in a soft, sincere voice, "I can't tell you how many times I've dreamed of that. But one of these days we'll find a way to get it back on the map."

"Hey, listen," McQueen said thoughtfully, "thanks for the drive. I had a great time. It's kind of nice to slow down every once in a while."

"You're welcome," Sally said, smiling.

The two cars headed back to town in silence, enjoying the view.

When they got back to town, Mater pulled up alongside McQueen.

"Hey, hey," Mater whispered, "if anyone asks you, we were out smashin' mailboxes, okay?" The tow truck tore off.

Just then, McQueen heard a noise. The ground was vibrating. And something was . . . mooing?

It was a tractor stampede—and it was heading straight for him!

McQueen ducked out of the tractors' path just in time. The stampede rolled downtown, where Ramone was busy painting the white divider line down the newest stretch of asphalt.

"Oh, man," Ramone groaned as he scurried away, "the paint's still wet!"

Red was watering his flowers at the base of the

Stanley statue. As the tractors drew near, he steeled himself to face the beasts. There was no way he was going to let a bunch of tractors take out his newly replanted posies!

The fire truck unleashed a mighty blast, and the tractors stopped in their tracks. With a group moo, they tipped over, except for a few strays who scattered in different directions.

"No, no, no, get out of the store!" Luigi cried frantically as his tire shop was overrun by stray tractors. "Hey! Don't eat the radial! Here, take the snow tire!"

"Mater!" Sheriff bellowed.

"I wasn't tractor-tippin'!" Mater insisted.

"Then where did all of these gol' dern tractors come from?" Sheriff demanded.

McQueen stood at the edge of town, smiling at the crazy tractors. Suddenly, he noticed one heading out of town. "Hey, guys?" he called. "There's one going this way. . . . I got it." He headed off to wrangle the tractor, following it all the way to Willys Butte. McQueen whistled. "Come here, come here, tractor." He followed it to the edge of the rise that overlooked the butte. "Don't wander off." Catching sight of a lone car at the butte, McQueen grew quiet. It was Doc. "What are you doing with those old racing tires?" McQueen muttered to himself. He snuck behind some brush to see what Doc was going to do.

Down below, Doc rubbed the dirt with a tire and sighed.

"Come on, Doc," McQueen whispered, eager to see the Hornet in action. "Drive."

Doc got into position, focusing on the track ahead. He took a moment to blow the carbon out of his pipes, then took off.

"Whoa!" McQueen said as Doc ripped down the straightaway, kicking up plumes of dust behind him. McQueen watched nervously as Doc charged the turn at full speed, but the old car countersteered, taking the curve beautifully. Finally, Doc finished the course and skidded to a stop in the same place he'd started. He was out of breath but smiling.

"Wow," McQueen said, driving up to Doc. "You're amazing!"

Doc's expression hardened. He hadn't realized

that anyone was watching. Without a word, the old race car took off, throwing dirt into McQueen's grill.

"What are you doing?" McQueen coughed. He wasn't about to let Doc leave without a word. "Doc, wait!" The race car followed Doc back into town.

Doc rumbled into his office, slamming the door behind him, but McQueen caught it with a tire and forced his way in. "Doc, hold it. Seriously, your driving's incredible."

"Wonderful," Doc grumbled. "Now, go away."

"Hey, I mean it," McQueen insisted. "You've still got it!"

Doc glared at the young race car. "I'm asking you to leave."

"C'mon," McQueen begged. "I'm a race car. You're a much older race car, but under the hood, you and I are the same."

"We are not the same!" Doc bellowed, losing his usual cool. "Understand? Now, get out!" Doc drove to the door and held it open.

But McQueen didn't budge. "How could a car like you quit at the top of your game?"

"You think I quit?" Doc demanded. He yanked

a pull chain, clicking on an overhead light. Below it was a framed article. CRASH WIPES OUT HUDSON HORNET, the headline read, above a photo of a much younger Doc—wrecked on a racetrack infield.

"Right . . . ," McQueen said slowly as his racing history came back to him, "your big wreck in '54."

"They quit on *me*." Doc was silent for a moment. "When I finally got put together, I went back expecting a big welcome. You know what they said? 'You're history.' Moved right on to the next rookie standing in line." He looked carefully at the photograph. "There was a lot left in me. I never got a chance to show 'em. I keep that to remind me never to go back. I just never expected that that world would find me here."

"Hey, look, Doc," McQueen said, an edge in his voice, "I'm not them."

"Oh, yeah?" Doc demanded. "When is the last time you cared about something except yourself, hot rod? You name me one time, and I will take it all back."

McQueen hesitated. As much as he wanted to show the older car that he was wrong, he couldn't

come up with anything that would convince Doc—
or himself—otherwise.

"*Uh-huh,*" Doc said. "I didn't think so. These
are good folk around here who care about one
another. I don't want them depending on someone
they can't count on."

"Count on?" McQueen said. "You've been here
how long and your friends don't even know who
you are. Who's caring only about himself?"

"Just finish that road and get outta here,"
Doc said. He drove off, leaving McQueen alone
with his thoughts.

As the sun peeked over the mountains the next morning, Mater yawned, stretched, and drove out to the edge of the new road. Doc drove up next to him, and the two autos surveyed the blacktop. It reached into the horizon, as flat and even as a field of fresh snow.

"He's done," Mater said quietly. "He musta finished it while we were all sleepin'."

"Good riddance," Doc grumbled. As he drove away, he passed the rest of the townsfolk, who were gazing sadly at the road, thinking McQueen was gone.

"He's gone?" Flo asked.

"Well," Sarge said, trying to rally his friends and keep up a brave face, "we wouldn't want him to miss that race of his."

"Oh, dude," Ramone said to Sheriff, whose eyes were sparkling, "are you crying?"

"What?" Sheriff was choked up, but he didn't want the others to see what a big softy he was. "No, no, no!" he insisted. "I'm happy. I don't have to watch him every second of the day anymore. I'm glad he's gone."

Red burst into tears and drove away, knocking over Luigi's stack of tires—again.

"What's wrong with Red?" a voice asked. It was McQueen.

"Oh, he's just sad 'cause you left town," Mater explained, "and went to your big race to win the Piston Cup that you've always dreamed about your whole life and get that big ol' sponsor and that fancy helicopter you were talkin' about—"

"Lightning! There you are!" The townsfolk gathered around the race car, chattering happily.

"Wait a minute!" Mater said, the truth finally dawning on him. "*Aw,* I knew you wouldn't leave without saying good-bye." He gave McQueen a friendly punch with his tire.

"What are you doing here, son?" Sheriff

demanded. "You're gonna miss your race. Now, don't worry, I'll give you a police escort, and we'll make up the time."

"Thank you, Sheriff," McQueen said gratefully. "Well, you know, I can't go just yet." He smiled playfully.

The town looked at one another in confusion.

"Why not?" Sheriff asked.

"I'm not sure these tires can get me all the way to California," McQueen replied, glancing at Luigi and Guido.

"Pit stop?" Guido asked hopefully.

"Yeah," McQueen said. "Does anybody know what time Luigi's opens?"

"Oh-ho-ho!" Luigi said, laughing. "I can't believe it!" He quickly flipped over his CLOSED sign to read OPEN, and the two Italian cars rolled aside so that McQueen could come into their garage for a complete overhaul. "Four new tires?" Luigi cried, thrilled. "*Grazie,* Mr. Lightning, *grazie.*"

"Would you look at that?" Flo said as the townsfolk peered at McQueen through Luigi's freshly cleaned window.

"Our first real customer in years!" Luigi said as he secured McQueen in a lift. "I am filled with-a tears of ecstasy, for this is a most glorious day of my life."

"All right, Luigi, give me the best set of black walls you got," McQueen ordered.

The lift dropped sharply down. "No, no, no, no," Luigi said as he made his way to a special curtained-off section of the store. "You don't-a know what you want. Black wall tires, they blend into the pavement, but these—" He whipped back the curtain. "Whitewall tires—they say, 'Look at me! Here I am! *Loooove* me!'"

"All right," McQueen said mildly, "you're the expert. Oh, and don't forget the spare." And with that, Luigi and Guido got to work.

"Uh-huh-huh?" Luigi said with a grin as McQueen admired his new whitewalls in a three-way mirror. "What did Luigi tell you, eh?"

"Wow, you were right," McQueen admitted, smiling at his flashy new tires. "Better than a Ferrari, huh?"

Luigi's smile evaporated. "Eh, no."

McQueen decided he'd better check out all the stores in town. "Wow," he said as he tasted some of Fillmore's organic fuel. "This organic fuel is great! Why haven't I heard about it before?"

"It's a conspiracy, man!" Fillmore shouted. "The oil companies got a grip on the government. They're feeding us a bunch of lies, man!"

"Okay," McQueen said slowly. "I'll take a case!"

Next, he went to Sarge's Surplus Hut and picked out some night-vision goggles for his drive to California. Then he chose a few Radiator Springs bumper stickers from Lizzie's memorabilia shop. At Ramone's, he got a snazzy new paint job—with a brand-new lightning bolt design. "Yeah!" McQueen said, laughing as he looked at the fresh paint. *"Ka-chow!"*

When Sally saw McQueen later that day, she couldn't believe his makeover. He was sparkling and detailed to perfection.

"Ka-pow!" McQueen said, showing off his new look. "What do you think? Radiator Springs looks pretty good on me."

Sally laughed. "I'll say!" She checked out his

new paint job. *"Ka-chow!"* she said admiringly.

"You're gonna fit right in, in California," she continued, looking at him all the while.

Suddenly, Sally realized something. "Oh my goodness, it looks like you've helped everybody in town."

"Yeah, everybody except one. . . . ," McQueen said, cuing the town to light up their signs. One by one, the lights flickered on.

"They fixed their neon," Sally said quietly, taking in the beauty of the town.

"Just like in its heyday, right?" McQueen said.

Sally sighed. "It's even better than I pictured it. Thank you."

Just then, Flo pulled onto the brand-new street. "Low and slow?" she said to Ramone.

"Oh, yeah," he agreed, and in the next moment, he and his wife were cruising down the strip. The two cars snuggled close, happier than they had been in years.

McQueen tried to take Sally for a cruise, but Lizzie stole him away.

"Lizzie!" Sally said in protest.

Mater was right there. "Miss Sally, may I have this cruise?" he asked.

Sally smiled. "Of course."

McQueen tried to dodge away from Lizzie, but she wouldn't let him escape her.

"I remember when Stanley first asked me to take a drive with him," she said, reminiscing.

McQueen was wondering how he could get to Sally when Mater towed him away. Lizzie happily continued to talk to herself.

"Hey!" McQueen said as he finally found himself next to Sally.

"Thanks, Mater," Sally said to the tow truck.

"Good evenin', you two." Mater gave Sally a broad wink, then drove off backward.

Just as McQueen and Sally were about to start cruising, Flo pulled up to them. She was looking at the horizon.

"Is that what I think it is?" she asked.

A wall of headlights was coming straight in their direction.

"Customers?" Sally asked.

"Customers!" Flo cried, her voice edged with

excitement. The town looked great. Maybe this was finally their big chance to get back on the map. "Customers, everybody, and a lot of 'em. You know what to do. Just like we rehearsed."

Suddenly, a helicopter roared overhead, sweeping a light across the town.

"It's the ghost light!" Mater cried. Terrified, he drove away.

"We have found McQueen!" blasted a voice from a PA system. "We have found McQueen!"

In a moment, the town was swarmed with reporters, photographers, and camera vans. The reporters jostled Sally out of the way as they descended onto McQueen, asking him questions a mile a minute.

One reporter barked, "Did you have a nervous breakdown, McQueen?"

"Look, McQueen's wearing whitewalls!"

"Are your tires prematurely balding?"

"Stickers?" Sally called. "McQueen?" But her voice was lost in the confusion of the crowd.

"McQueen!" shouted a TV reporter. "Will you still race for the Piston Cup?"

"Sally?" McQueen called. "Sally? Sally!" He searched for the Porsche, but he couldn't find her in the chaos.

Just then, a truck horn blared. It was Mack! He drove toward McQueen, shoving reporters out of his way.

"You're here!" Mack cried. His voice was thick with tears. "Thank the manufacturers you're alive! Oh, you are a sight for sore headlights. I'm so sorry I lost you, boss. I'll make it up to you."

Mack unhooked the trailer and held back the press so that McQueen could get inside.

"Mack," McQueen said in a dazed voice, "I can't believe you're here."

"Is that the world's fastest racing machine?" boomed a familiar voice.

"Is that Harv?" McQueen asked.

"Yeah, he's in the back," Mack replied.

Then Mack turned to the reporters. "Get back, you oil-thirsty parasites!"

"Harv!" McQueen called into the trailer. "Harv?"

"Kid! I'm over here."

A speakerphone slid easily from the side of the trailer.

"How ya doin', buddy?" McQueen asked into the microphone.

"I'm doing great!" Harv exclaimed. "You're everywhere—radio, TV, the papers. What do you need me for?"

Then the agent's voice turned serious. "That's just a figure of speech. You signed a contract. Where are you? I can't even find you on my GPS."

"I'm in this little town called Radiator Springs," McQueen explained excitedly. "You know Highway Sixty-six? It's still here!"

"Yeah, great, kiddo," Harv said, cutting off McQueen. "Playtime is over, pal. While the world's been tryin' to find you, Dinoco's had nobody to woo. Who they gonna woo?"

McQueen knew the answer to that one. "Chick."

"Bingo," Harv said. "Mack, roll the tape."

The TV screen glowed blue, showing footage of Chick standing next to Tex Dinoco. Chick was surrounded by reporters and gorgeous female fans. He even had a new dark thundercloud with a giant *C* painted on him.

"Show us the thunder!" the reporters begged.

"Yeah, give us the thundercloud!"

"You want thunder?" Chick demanded, basking

in the attention. "You want thunder? *Ka-chick-a! Ka-chick-a! Ka-chick-a!*"

"Hey," McQueen said in horror, "that's my bit!"

"You gotta get to Cali pronto," Harv yelled. "Just get out of Radiation Stinks now, or Dinoco is history, you hear me?"

"Yeah, okay," McQueen said slowly, "just give me a second here, Harv." McQueen drove over to Sally, who was parked by the side of the trailer. They looked at each other in silence for a moment.

McQueen spoke first. "Sally, I—I want you to— look, I wish . . ." He sighed and looked at the ground. He didn't know what to say.

"Thank you," Sally said sincerely. "Thanks for everything."

McQueen looked up at her. "It was just a road."

"No—it was much more than that." Tears welled up in Sally's eyes.

Mack charged over, interrupting them. "We gotta go," he said. "Harv's going crazy. He's gonna have me fired if I don't get you in the truck now."

"Mack, just hold it," McQueen begged. He looked at Sally, pained.

"You should go," Sally told him.

McQueen started to speak, but Sally cut him off. "I hope you find what you're looking for," she told him. Then she backed away and turned, pushing through the press.

"Sally . . . ," McQueen called. "Sally!" But it was too late. She was gone.

"C'mon," Harv urged. "Let's go." The agent coaxed as McQueen backed into the trailer. "That's right, kid, let's go. You're a superstar. You don't belong there anyway."

McQueen looked out at the soft neon glow of the town lights one last time before the ramp shut behind him.

As Mack hauled McQueen out of town, the folks of Radiator Springs watched sadly. Just then, a reporter rolled up to Doc.

"Hey, are you Doc Hudson?" she asked. "Thanks for the call."

Sally's jaw dropped. "You did this?"

"It's best for everyone, Sally," Doc said.

"Best for everyone?" Sally demanded. "Or best for you?"

"Hey, guys!" shouted a reporter. "McQueen's leaving in the truck!"

The press raced after him, leaving the town as suddenly as they had arrived.

"I didn't get to say good-bye to him," Mater said sadly.

One by one, the townsfolk went back to their shops. Alone, Doc sat under the town's traffic light as they all turned off their neon. Radiator Springs was quiet and dark once again.

"**O**kay, here we go," McQueen said to himself as he sat idling in the darkness of the trailer. It was the day of the Piston Cup Championship, and McQueen was working hard to find the zone.

"Focus," he commanded himself. "Speed. I am speed."

Across the country, cars had closed up their shops and headed to the closest television set to watch the race of the century.

"Bob, there's a crowd of nearly three hundred thousand cars here at the Los Angeles International Speedway," Darrell said as he and Bob sat in the announcers' booth. "Tickets to this race are hotter than a black leather seat on a hot summer day."

Chick was feeling smug as he basked in the limelight. He was surrounded by press and photographers, soaking up all the attention.

"C'mon, Chick, let's see the cloud!" begged the reporters. "Flash that thunder, baby!"

"Oh, yeah, you wanna know the forecast?" Chick bragged. "I'll give you the forecast: one hundred percent chance of thunder! *Ka-chick-a! Ka-chick-a!* Say it with me!"

Meanwhile, McQueen stayed in his trailer, ignoring the chaos outside. He revved his engine. "Victory," he muttered quietly as he pictured himself flying down the track ahead of Chick and The King. "One winner, two losers. Speed. Speed. Speed!" McQueen remembered the drive with Sally and the view of Radiator Springs from the spot near the Wheel Well. *Gosh, that was gorgeous,* McQueen thought. He smiled a little, picturing the townsfolk. *I never even said good-bye to Mater,* he thought regretfully.

"Hey, Lightning!" Mack called as he banged on the trailer door. "You ready?"

McQueen's eyes snapped open. *What am I doing?* he thought. *I don't have time to daydream— I have a race to win!* "Yeah, yeah, yeah," he said, giving himself a good shake. "I'm ready."

He rolled out of his trailer and faced the enormous crowd of fans. They let out a deafening cheer, and McQueen squinted as a thousand cameras flashed in his face.

"Thanks for being my pit crew today," McQueen said to Mack, who was parked beside a big gas can.

"Least I could do," Mack replied.

Out on the track, a group of color-coded cars drove in formation, spelling out the words "Piston Cup."

In the announcers' booth, Bob explained that this would be the last race for Strip Weathers—The King.

"You know, Chick Hicks ain't gonna let The King just drive away with it today," Darrell added. "He's gonna pull out all the stops to win this one."

"And there he is," Bob said as the stadium monitor flashed an image of McQueen pulling up to the starting line. "Lightning McQueen. Missing all week and then he turns up in the middle of nowhere, in a little town called Radiator Springs."

"Wearing whitewall tires," Darrell added with a chuckle, "of all things."

Chick pulled up next to McQueen and flashed his shiny thundercloud. *"Ka-chick-a! Ka-chick-a! Ka-chick-a!"* He laughed uproariously. "Hey, where ya been, McQueen? I've been kind of lonely, nobody to hang out with—I mean, except the Dinoco folks."

Chick babbled on, but McQueen was having a hard time paying attention to him. His mind was wandering. He was back on the mountain with Sally. *Gee, she looked pretty that day,* McQueen thought as he pictured the beautiful Porsche in front of the waterfall.

Just then, the green flag dropped. Chick and The King were off like bullets.

"Uuuugh!" McQueen cried as he snapped out of his daydream. "Shoot!" He took off after them, chasing their bumpers. Two laps later, all three cars were battling for first place.

"Oh, Chick slammed the door on him," Darrell announced as Chick moved in to cut off McQueen. With a sudden burst of speed, Chick left the rookie in his dust.

"Chick's not making it easy on him today," Bob said. It was true. Although he wanted more than ever to win, McQueen was having trouble focusing on the race. His mind kept wandering. Like right then: he was picturing himself on the drive up the mountain with Sally again. He remembered how she had splashed him. And—

A wall!

McQueen jarred himself out of his memory just in time to swerve away from the concrete wall. But he cut too hard and spun deep into the infield. The crowed gasped.

Chick grinned. "Just me and the old man, fellas," he told his pit crew over the radio. "McQueen just doesn't have it today."

McQueen idled in the infield, dazed. He could hear The King and Chick speeding around the track—but they seemed far away.

"Kid, you all right?" Mack asked over the radio.

McQueen gave himself a shake, trying to clear his head. He knew that he was losing time. He'd never catch up to the other cars now. "Uh, Mack, I don't know. I don't think—"

Suddenly, a different—and familiar—voice growled over the radio. "I didn't come all this way to see you quit."

McQueen gasped. "Doc?" The rookie peered at pit row, where a crowd of folks were waving. Almost everyone was there—Ramone, Flo, Luigi, Guido, Fillmore, Sarge—even Mater. "Guys!" McQueen cried happily. "You're here!"

"Hey, it was Doc's idea, man," Ramone said.

McQueen looked at the crew chief platform. Doc was there—painted up as the Fabulous Hudson Hornet. He looked glorious. "I knew you needed a crew chief," Doc rumbled, "but I didn't know it was this bad."

"Doc, look at you!" McQueen said in awe. "I thought you said you'd never come back."

"Well, I really didn't have a choice," Doc replied. "Mater didn't get to say good-bye."

"Good-bye!" Mater hollered. He looked at Doc. "Okay, I'm good."

McQueen laughed.

"All right," Doc said, getting down to business, "if you can drive as good as you can fix a road, then you can win this race with your eyes shut. Now, get back out there."

In an instant, McQueen tore onto the track. Suddenly, he felt he had the focus of a laser beam. The team from Radiator Springs let out a cheer as he ripped up the asphalt, gaining on Chick and The King.

"We are back in business!" Doc shouted. "Guido,

Luigi—you're going up against professional pit crews, boys. You're gonna have to be fast."

"They will not know what hit them!" Luigi promised.

"Kid, you can beat these guys," Doc said over his headset. "Find the groove that works for you and get those laps back!"

Meanwhile, the monitors showed McQueen's new crew. "Darrell, it appears McQueen has got himself a pit crew," Bob said as the cameras zoomed in on Doc, "and look who he has for a crew chief."

The crowd recognized Doc and began to cheer, welcoming him back.

Bob looked down at pit row in amazement. "Wow, this is history in the making; nobody has seen the racing legend in over fifty years."

But history was happening on the track, too, as McQueen whipped past Chick and The King.

"McQueen's coming up fast. . . . He goes three wide and passes them on the inside!" Bob announced excitedly. He couldn't believe it.

"What?" Chick was shocked as McQueen slid

past, making up the first of his two lost laps.

Back in Radiator Springs, Sally, Lizzie, and Red watched McQueen on television.

"C'mon! You got it, Stickers!" Sally exclaimed.

Making up his second lap, McQueen closed in on Chick and The King again.

"Oh," Chick muttered, "kid's just trying to be a hero, huh?" With a sudden jerk, Chick knocked McQueen as he started to pass. "Well, what do you think of this?" He sneered as McQueen spun around until he was facing backward.

But McQueen didn't slow down. He bolted past Chick—in reverse.

"Whoa!" Mater whooped from pit row. "I taught him that. *Ka-chow!*"

"What a move by McQueen!" Bob cried as he looked down on the race from the booth. "He's caught up to the leaders!"

"A three-way battle for the lead with ten to go," Darrell continued.

McQueen was giving the race everything he had. He was tight on Chick's tail, but Chick was doing everything in his power to block McQueen. There was the grind of scraping metal as the two cars rubbed together. "No, you don't—" Chick snarled.

Just then, one of McQueen's tires popped. "Doc, I'm flat," he cried. "I'm flat!"

"Bring it in," Doc commanded as the yellow flag dropped, signaling that there was debris on the track. That meant the race was temporarily suspended; the other cars had to slow down and follow the pace car while the mess was removed. "Don't tear yourself up, kid."

Doc knew that they had to get McQueen back onto the track before the pace car came around. Otherwise, McQueen would fall behind again.

"Guido!" Doc shouted. "It's time."

"Hey, tiny," one of Chick's pitties teased, "you gonna clean his windshield?"

Chick's pitties cracked up as McQueen pulled in. But Guido ignored them. This was his life dream— to give the ultimate pit stop. And he was ready.

In one fluid movement, Guido tossed the tires into the air and bolted them onto McQueen before they could hit the ground.

Guido looked at Chick's stunned pit crew and blew on his torque gun. Then he offered the only English he knew. "Pit stop."

"Guido, you did it!" Luigi cried as McQueen pulled back onto the track, moving into place behind the pace car.

"Did you see that, Bob?" Darrell cried from the announcers' booth.

Bob gaped in awe. "That was the fastest pit stop I've ever seen!"

On the track, the green flag dropped, and the three cars surged forward, racing at a furious pace.

"This is it!" Bob announced with excitment. "We're heading into the final lap and McQueen is right behind the leaders. What a comeback!"

"This is it, kiddo," Doc said as McQueen closed in on Chick and The King. "You got four turns left. One at a time. Drive it in deep and hope it sticks."

His eyes narrowed in determination, McQueen headed toward the first turn.

"Go!" Doc cried, and McQueen did.

He pushed everything he had into high gear. Seeing his rival make his move, Chick cut quickly to bash McQueen against a wall. But McQueen was too fast; Chick missed him.

But Chick didn't slow down. Instead, he drove forward, ramming his front bumper into McQueen's rear. McQueen spun wildly toward the infield.

But McQueen wasn't about to give up. At the last moment, he cut right to go left, just the way Doc had taught him. With a smooth swerve, he shot back onto the track—in the lead!

"McQueen has taken the lead!" Darrell announced to the audience. "Lightning McQueen is going to win the Piston Cup!"

Chick and The King had fallen behind McQueen. But Chick wasn't giving up, either. If he couldn't win, he could at least come in second. "I'm not coming in behind you again, old man!" he cried as he rammed The King, causing The King to spin into the wall.

Crash!

The crowd gasped as The King stopped in the infield, battered, dented, and unable to move.

McQueen was moving toward the finish line when he heard the boos. Confused, he looked at the giant television monitor and saw The King. He wasn't moving. An image of Doc flashed into McQueen's mind: Doc had looked the same way in the photo of the Fabulous Hudson Hornet's famous crash.

McQueen screeched to a stop right before the finish line.

"Yeah!" Chick hollered as he shot past McQueen. "Woo-hoo! I won, baby! Yeah! Oh, yeah! Woo-hoo-hoo!"

"What's he doing, Doc?" Flo whispered as she watched McQueen. He was inches from the finish line and still hadn't moved.

Suddenly, McQueen put himself into reverse and

headed back toward where The King had come to a stop.

"What are you doing, kid?" The King asked as McQueen approached. He was completely wiped out, but not completely broken; McQueen could see that.

"I think The King should finish his last race," McQueen said humbly. And then, as gently as he could, McQueen began to push The King toward the finish line.

"You just gave up the Piston Cup," The King pointed out, "you know that?"

"Ah, this grumpy old race car I know once told me something," McQueen said as he helped The King to the end of the track. "It's just an empty cup." Doc smiled proudly as he listened on his radio.

Meanwhile, Chick was hooting in triumph, turning doughnuts in the infield. "Woo-hoo-hoo!" It took him a moment to realize that no one was cheering with him. In fact, no one was even watching him. "Hey, what?" He stopped in his tracks. "What's going on?"

McQueen pushed The King across the finish

line, and the crowd erupted in cheers! The stadium went crazy at the sight of one of the proudest moments in racing history.

"Way to go, buddy!" Mater hollered.

Fillmore teared up a little. "There's a lot of love out there, you know, man?"

"Don't embarrass me, Fillmore," Sarge grunted.

The only one who wasn't impressed was Chick. He raced onto the winner's platform impatiently. "Come on, baby," he said. "Bring it out, bring out the Piston Cup. *Ka-chick-a! Ka-chick-a!*"

But nobody came out to deliver the cup. Instead, someone tossed it onto the stage, where it clattered to the floor beside Chick. No one cheered.

"Now, that's what I'm talking about right there, yeah!" Chick crowed. He looked around at the silent spectators. "Hey, how come the only one celebrating is me, huh? Where are the girls? Come on, where's the fireworks? Bring on the confetti!"

A confetti cannon let out a shot and hit Chick's bumper hard. "*Owww!* Hey, easy with the confetti. What's going on? Come on, snap some cameras, let's wrap this up. I gotta go sign my deal with

Dinoco," Chick said, starting to realize that no one cared.

The crowd started to boo.

"What's wrong with everybody?" Chick demanded as a few of the cars started throwing garbage onto the stage. "Hey! Hey! This is the start of the Chick era!" Chick finally gave up, grabbed his Piston Cup, and scampered away.

But McQueen didn't pay attention to any of that. He was too busy pushing The King toward the Dinoco tent. Then, as The King's wife hurried over to give her husband a kiss, McQueen quietly headed to the Rust-eze tent. His whole pit crew had gathered there—along with the goofy brothers from Rust-eze, who had given McQueen his start in racing.

"You made us proud, kid," one of the brothers said affectionately.

"Congrats on the loss, me bucko," Mack said.

Doc smiled at the younger race car. "You got a lotta stuff, kid."

"Thanks, Doc."

"Hey, Lightning!" Tex Dinoco called from the

front of the Dinoco tent. "How about comin' over here and talking to me a minute?"

McQueen drove over to join him.

"Son, that was some real racin' out there," Tex said to McQueen. "How'd you like to become the new face of Dinoco?"

McQueen looked up at the fancy Dinoco tent area. The helicopter gave him a wink.

"But I didn't win," McQueen pointed out.

"Lightnin'," Tex went on, "there's a whole lot more to racin' than just winnin'."

McQueen was tempted. It was everything he had always dreamed of. Dinoco was a great company with a lot of money. And Tex seemed like a really great guy. Still . . . McQueen looked at the Rust-eze tent, where the two brothers were telling their usual lousy jokes He couldn't help smiling.

"Thank you, Mr. Tex," McQueen told the mogul, "but those Rust-eze guys over there gave me my big break. I think I'm gonna stick with them."

"Well, I sure can respect that," Tex said sincerely. "Still, you know, if there's ever anything I can do for you, just let me know."

"I sure appreciate that. Thank you." McQueen thought for a moment. "Actually," he said, "there is *one* thing."

"*Woo-hoo!*" Mater hollered, leaning out the window of the Dinoco helicopter as it flew over the Wheel Well. "Hey, hey! Hey, look at me! I'm flyin'!"

It was two days later, and Radiator Springs was hopping. A glistening red Ferrari and two black Maseratis had just rolled into Luigi's tire shop.

"So," the Ferrari told Luigi, "Lightning McQueen told me this was the best place in the world to get tires. How about setting me and my friends up with three or four sets each?"

Luigi gasped. It was Michael Schumacher! "Guido . . . ," he cried. "There is a real Michael Schumacher Ferrari in-a my store! A real Ferrari! Punch me, Guido! Punch me in the face. This is the most glorious day of my life!"

Luigi fainted in their presence.

The Ferrari turned to Guido. "I hope your little friend's okay," he said in Italian. "I hear wonderful things about your store."

Guido gaped at the Ferrari. Then he fainted, too.

Sally was at the Wheel Well, looking down on the town, when McQueen appeared beside her. He was decked out in his full Radiator Springs paint and stickers.

"*Ka-chow!*" he said.

They both laughed.

"Just passin' through?" Sally asked.

"Actually . . . ," McQueen said, keeping his voice casual, "I thought I'd stop and stay a while." He leaned toward Sally. "I hear this place is back on the map," he said in a confidential whisper.

Sally gave him a dubious look. "It is?"

"Yeah, there's a rumor floating around that some hotshot Piston Cup race car is setting up his big racing headquarters here," McQueen replied.

Sally's eyes widened. "Really?" she asked, then caught herself. "Oh, well . . . ," she said, playing it cool. "There goes the town."

"You know," McQueen whispered, "I really missed you, Sally." The race car leaned closer to her.

"McQueen and Sally, parked beneath a tree!" Mater shouted as the helicopter flew past.

"K-I-S-S . . . uh . . . I-N-T!"

"Great timing, Mater!" McQueen shouted. He looked at Sally. "He's my best friend. . . . ," he explained with a shrug. "What are you gonna do?"

"So, Stickers," Sally said, giving him a playful grin. "Last one to Flo's buys?"

"I don't know, why don't we just take a drive?" McQueen suggested.

Sally's eyes twinkled. "Naah." Then she suddenly took off down the mountain.

"Yeah!" McQueen shouted as he took off after her. *"Ka-chow!"*